To future president Eliza Taylor-Berry, who inspired this story, and
to the wonderful folks at Wonderland Books in Rockford, Illinois —A.R.

To a great pal, Nina Frenkel —S.V.

Library of Congress Cataloging-in-Publication Data:

Reynolds, Aaron, 1970- author.
President Squid / by Aaron Reynolds ; illustrated by Sara Varon.
pages cm
Summary: A giant squid decides that he has the right stuff to be President Squid.
ISBN 978-1-4521-3647-9
1. Giant squids—Juvenile fiction. 2. Presidents—Juvenile fiction.
[1. Giant squids—Fiction. 2. Squids—Fiction. 3. Presidents—Fiction. 4. Humorous stories.]
I. Varon, Sara, illustrator. II. Title.

PZ7.R33213Pr 2016
[E]—dc23
2014022142

Manufactured in China.

Design by Kristine Brogno.
Typeset in Berliner Grotesk.
The illustrations in this book were rendered in
ink & brush on bristol paper and colored in Photoshop.

10 9 8 7 6 5 4 3 2 1

Chronicle Books LLC
680 Second Street
San Francisco, California 94107

Chronicle Books—we see things differently.
Become part of our community at www.chroniclekids.com.

PRESIDENT SQUID

vote for Squid!

by
Aaron Reynolds

illustrated by
Sara Varon

chronicle books · san francisco

I HAVE REALIZED SOMETHING VERY IMPORTANT.

Something that changes everything!

No giant squid has ever been president before!

Which means I will be the first.

President Squid!

Now *that* has a nice ring to it.

← me!

I WILL BE THE GREATEST PRESIDENT WHO EVER LIVED!

Reason #1:
Presidents WEAR TIES.

See? Tie!

See? Tie!

See? Tie!

Bowties count.

Wearing a tie is
VERY presidential.
And I look fabulous in a tie.
Do you see any other giant squids
around here wearing ties?

That's what
I thought.

Reason #2:
The president has the
BIGGEST HOUSE EVER.

Have you seen the president's house?

It's huge! I mean, this place is ENORMOUS!

Well, have you seen my house?

It's not just huge. It's not just enormous.

It's absolutely TITANIC!

Pretty cool, huh?

Reason #3:
Presidents are FAMOUS.

Let's face it . . .

I'm the most famous sea creature

on this whole page!

Do you know that guy?

Of course not. He's a nobody.

How about that fish over there?

You never heard of him, right?

How about me? Do you know who I am?

President Squid, you say?

EXACTLY! I even have a book named after me!

You're reading it right now!

See? Famous.

Reason #4:
Presidents get to do
ALL THE TALKING.

I'm great at doing all the talking. I'm doing all the talking

right now. I'm doing all the talking about

"Five Reasons Why I Should Be President."

And when presidents talk . . . everyone has to listen.

Are you listening?

I said, "EVERYONE HAS TO LISTEN!"

And finally, Reason #5:

The president is the BIG BOSS.

Bossing people around may be the most presidential thing a president does.

And I'm perfect at being the big boss.

After all, there's nobody bigger than me!

See?

And there's nobody bossier than me!

Hey, Shark! Brush your teeth!

Hey, Jellyfish! Comb your tentacles! You look terrible!

See? Very bossy.

I'LL BE IN CHARGE OF EVERYBODY!!!

I think I'm ready for all that power.

Let's go over this once more,
for those of you who
are a little slow.

Wears a tie? Check.

Huge house? Check.

Famous? Check.

Does all the talking? Check-checkity-check-check.

Big and bossy? Check. And check.

I'm PERFECT for this job!

ALL HAIL PRESIDENT SQUID!

I said,
"ALL HAIL
PRESIDENT
SQUID!"

There is no hailing going on.

What's the problem, people?

CLAM, THIS IS PRESIDENT SQUID!

I do all the talking, yessiree bob!

When I talk, EVERYBODY has to listen!

Presidents talk, clams listen—that's my motto!

I say, "Swim"; you say, "How fast?"!

I say, "Back off from the sardine";

you back off, bub!

And I say unhand him!

THIS VERY INSTANT!

Clams don't have ears.

Wait!

I have realized something very important.

Being president is exhausting.

I do not want to be president.

I want to be . . .

KING SQUID! ALL-POWERFUL RULER OF THE ENTIRE UNIVERSE!

Now *that* has a nice ring to it.